Samson
&
Ryan

Larry

Benny

© 2006 Disney Enterprises, Inc.
All rights reserved.

Published by Scholastic Inc., 90 Old Sherman Turnpike, Danbury, Connecticut 06816.

No part of this publication may be reproduced in whole or in part, or stored in a retrieval
system, or transmitted in any form or by any means, electronic, mechanical, photocopying,
recording, or otherwise, without written permission of the copyright holder.

SCHOLASTIC and associated logos are trademarks
and/or registered trademarks of Scholastic Inc.

For information regarding permission, write to:
Disney Licensed Publishing, 114 Fifth Avenue, New York, New York 10011.

0-7172-8660-6

Printed in the U.S.A.
First printing, July 2006

Disney's
THE WILD

SCHOLASTIC INC.

New York   Toronto   London   Auckland   Sydney
Mexico City   New Delhi   Hong Kong   Buenos Aires

Samson the lion loved telling stories about the Wild to his son, Ryan. Their friends at the zoo—Bridget the giraffe, Larry the snake, and Nigel the koala—had heard these stories, too. Even Benny the squirrel knew all about Samson's exciting adventures in Africa.

"He was the biggest wildebeest I had ever seen," Samson was telling everyone.

Ryan rolled his eyes. He had heard this story many times before.

The cub wanted to be just like his brave father. But Ryan had been born at the zoo. His father thought the zoo was a great place, but Ryan didn't.

Ryan wished he could go to the Wild, so he could learn to roar like his father. Then his father would be proud of him. Inspired by his father's story, the cub opened his mouth to let out a loud roar. But it was more of a funny squeak.

The zoo visitors laughed. Ryan felt terrible!

Soon it was time for the zoo to close. But the animals didn't settle down for the night.

That's because this was the night of the big game. It was the penguins against Samson's team in the turtle curling championship.

All the animals went to the
penguin enclosure—all except Ryan.

Samson wasn't playing well because Ryan wasn't there. It looked like the penguins might win!

"We will not lose to flightless birds," Bridget stated.

Samson agreed. "We're going to use the secret play."

Using Larry the snake as a big slingshot, Samson shot the turtle—and it looked as if it was going to stop right on the bull's-eye . . .

. . . until the ground started to shake, ruining Samson's shot. The shaking was caused by a gazelle stampede that had been started accidentally by Ryan and his friends.

Then the gazelles ran into the penguin enclosure. What a mess!

Ryan was very sorry. Samson was angry and disappointed. This made Ryan feel worse. He was never going to be able to make his father proud of him now.

The sad cub went for a walk. He spotted some big green boxes on the other side of the zoo's fence.

Earlier, some pigeons had told him that these boxes were being shipped to the Wild.

Suddenly Ryan had a great idea. He would hide inside one of the boxes and sail away to the Wild. Then he would return to the zoo with a mighty roar! His dad was sure to be proud of him then!

Ryan made his way over the fence and curled up inside a box.

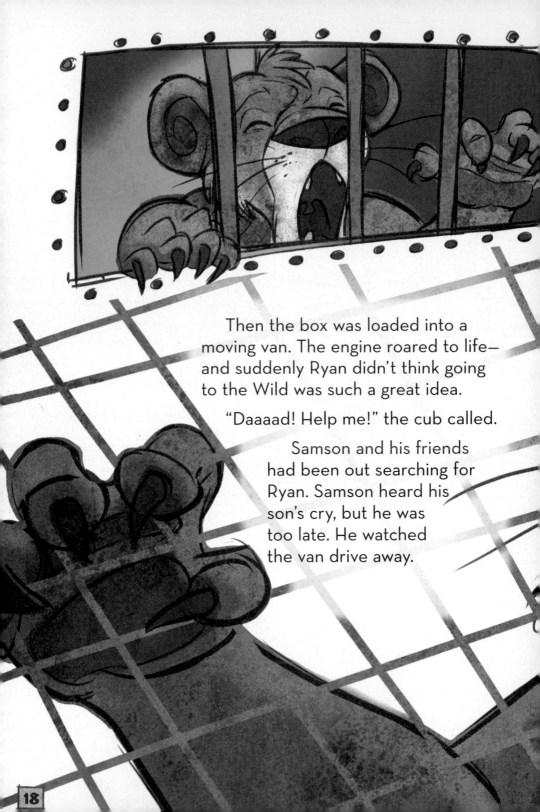

Then the box was loaded into a moving van. The engine roared to life— and suddenly Ryan didn't think going to the Wild was such a great idea.

"Daaaad! Help me!" the cub called.

Samson and his friends had been out searching for Ryan. Samson heard his son's cry, but he was too late. He watched the van drive away.

So Samson, Bridget, Nigel, Benny, and Larry set out to rescue Ryan. They had to sneak out of the zoo and make their way to the big water before Ryan's box was loaded onto a ship.

First they hid themselves in a garbage truck that was leaving the zoo. Benny the squirrel was sure he could lead them through the city to the big water. "Couple lefts, couple rights, bada-boom . . . you're there," he told his friends.

Then Benny
fell off the truck!

When the truck stopped, the animals managed
to get out. They wandered the streets of New York,
staring at the skyscrapers and bright neon lights.
But without Benny, they were lost.

They ended up in the city's sewers.
Luckily, the resident crocodiles thought
they were tourists. The crocodiles happily
gave the visitors directions to the big water.

But when they reached the water they were too late. They watched as Ryan's box was loaded onto a ship. Before Samson could reach the ship, it sailed away.

"We've got to follow that ship!" Samson cried. There was a boat docked nearby. The animals jumped onboard. The captain jumped overboard!

The animals managed to launch the boat and sail after Ryan. But they weren't very good sailors. They were almost lost at sea.

Luckily, Benny arrived with a flock of
Canadian geese. Since Canadian geese are
travel experts, they were able to lead Samson
and his friends to Ryan's ship.

They followed Ryan's ship for days and days
until their boat finally landed . . .

. . . on the shore of a tropical
island. They had reached the Wild!
The animals looked at Samson.
But the lion didn't know what to
do next—because he wasn't really
from the Wild after all!

Samson admitted that he had made up
all of his stories about the Wild.

"I'm a fraud, okay? I'm sorry. Just go back to the boat. I can't protect you out here," Samson said to his friends.

Once they knew they were unprotected in the Wild, Samson's friends panicked. They raced back to the boat. Samson headed into the jungle alone to find Ryan.

But Benny convinced the others to stay and help Samson. "I know you're scared," the squirrel said. "But Sammy's out there all alone. And so is Ryan."

Bravely, the animals headed out into the jungle—and right into trouble. They were soon surrounded by wildebeests. The scary animals scooped up Nigel and forced the rest of the gang into a dark cave in the base of a volcano.

The wildebeests treated Nigel like a king. They put him on a throne and placed a crown on his head.

Nigel was confused.

Then Kazar, the leader of the wildebeests, stepped forward. "Oh, Great Him," Kazar said to Nigel. "You must lead us in our transformation from prey to predator." It seemed that the wildebeests thought Nigel was a god who would teach them how to eat lions! And for practice, the wildebeests wanted to start by eating Nigel's friends!

Meanwhile, Samson had finally found a sign of Ryan—he heard his son calling for help.

Ryan was being chased by two vultures. But when Samson arrived, the vultures quickly flew off.

"Dad!" Ryan shouted happily. It felt good to be together once again.

But their happiness was cut short when Kazar's wildebeests arrived.

"Run, Son!" shouted Samson. Then he pushed his son up a tree and climbed up after him.

"Dad, you should be chasing them away," a confused Ryan told his father.

So Samson told his son the truth. Samson had really been born in a circus. But because he couldn't roar, he had been shipped off to a zoo in disgrace.

"I wanted you to be proud of me," Samson said, trying to explain why he had made up the stories.

Ryan was hurt because his father had lied to him.

Suddenly the wildebeests attacked! They rammed into the tree, toppling it. Ryan fell to the ground, but Samson went over a giant cliff!

The wildebeests forced Ryan to go to the dark cave inside the volcano.

Ryan was happy to see his old friends, but not for long. Kazar was now ready to eat the zoo gang and the lion cub!

Nigel had to do something—but what? Stalling for time, Nigel issued a command. "We cannot cook them without onions," he said.

Samson appeared in the nick of time. The volcano was beginning to rumble as the wildebeests surrounded the lions. Then the wildebeests stopped.

"We're tired of pretending to be something we're not," one of the wildebeests said to Kazar. They didn't want to eat anyone.

"Fine," said Kazar, "I'll kill them myself." Kazar quickly knocked Samson to the ground.

"He's going to kill Samson if we don't do something," Benny shouted.

"Why don't we use the secret play?" Larry suggested.

So the friends launched Ryan at Kazar. He let out a giant *ROAR* as he sailed at the evil wildebeest. But Kazar tossed the cub to the ground.

"Get away from my son," bellowed Samson. He let out a mighty *ROAR* that sent Kazar flying into the cave wall. The noise shook the walls and rocks rained down on Kazar.

But when Samson stopped roaring, the shaking continued. The volcano was about to erupt!

Luckily, everyone got out in time.

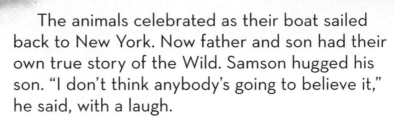

The animals celebrated as their boat sailed back to New York. Now father and son had their own true story of the Wild. Samson hugged his son. "I don't think anybody's going to believe it," he said, with a laugh.

But it didn't matter. Father and son would always be proud of who they really were—and proud of each other.

THE END

45

EYE SPY

Go on an adventure.
Look back in the story
and find these
wild pictures.